How to Catch an Elf

Adam Wallace

Andy Elkerton

SCHOLASTIC INC.

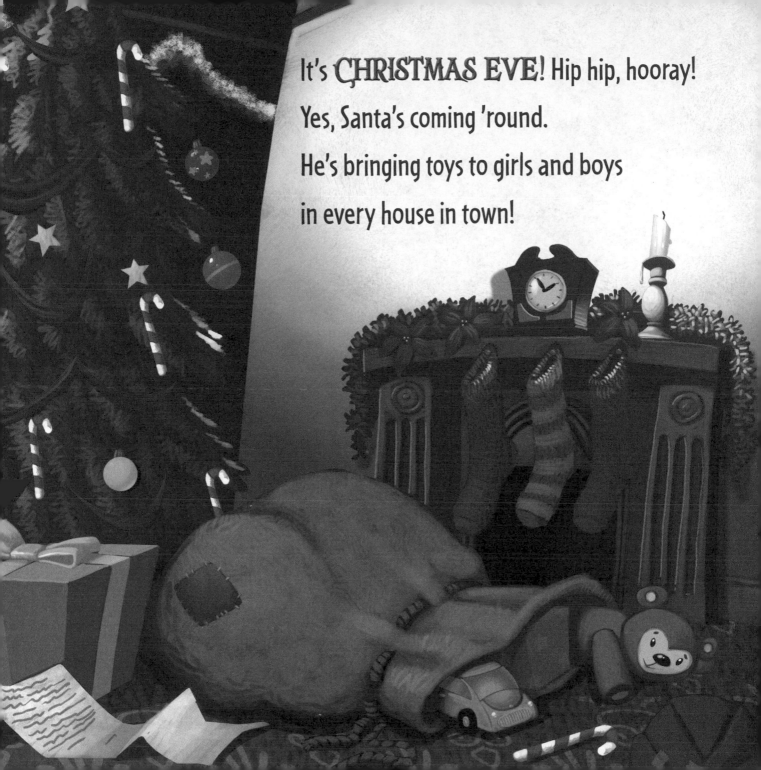

It's CHRISTMAS EVE! Hip hip, hooray!
Yes, Santa's coming 'round.
He's bringing toys to girls and boys
in every house in town!

Some kids have tried to catch him,
but Santa's fast, you see!
So they've set their eyes on a smaller prize,
and now they're after **me!**

Now Santa's ready—time to go.

I'm sure your traps are **SCARY!**

I'll do my best to dodge them all

and leave you feeling merry!

In I go, to Emma's house,
to make sure all is clear.
A TINSEL net? Oh, that's just fun!
I won't get caught in here!

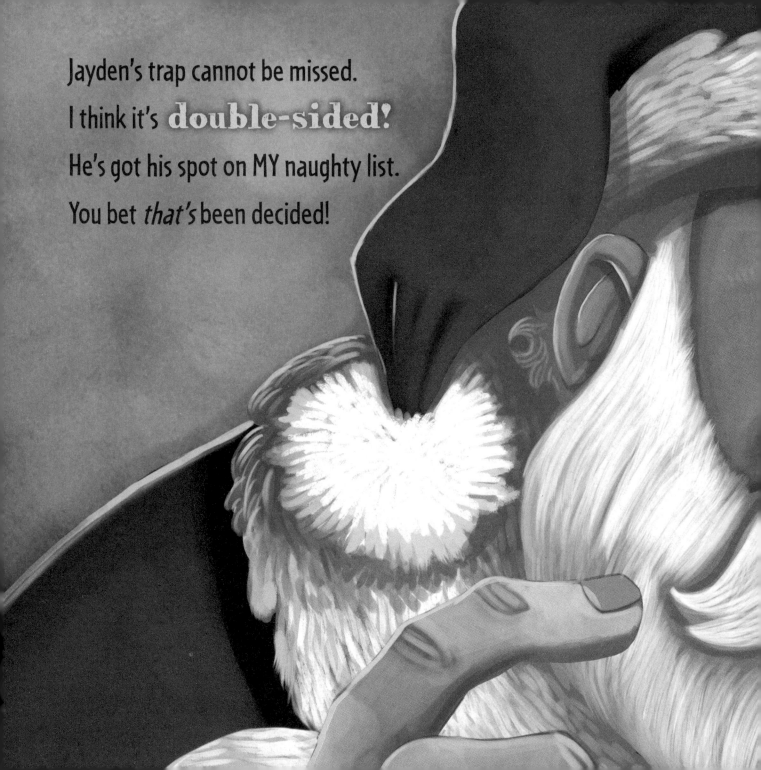

Jayden's trap cannot be missed.
I think it's **double-sided!**
He's got his spot on MY naughty list.
You bet *that's* been decided!

Another house is filled with treats.

These kids are getting smarter!

I can't resist the *candy canes.*

My job is getting harder!

Santa slowly lowers me
into a dangerous room.
If I touch down, he won't just frown . . .
there'll be a bonbon **BOOM!**

SNIP

Your Christmas maze is all laid out.
My work's no longer cushy.
I safely brought you all your gifts,
but, HEY, you ZAPPED my tushy!

And now my radar's PERKING UP!

This next one's quite a chore.

We don't yet know what lies ahead

in this family grocery store.

We run inside and get caught up
in an AVALANCHE of food!
We've seen all kinds of traps before,
but not to this magnitude!

THE *DINNER CANNON*™ burps and spits
and shoots out ham and gravy!
And then it follows with dessert?!
Please, Santa, will you save me?

We tumble down the waterfall
above the eggnog river,
but Santa and I are an AWESOME team...

Together, we deliver!

And now it's time for us to leave.

Our night is nearly done.

You tried your best this Christmas Eve,

so . . .

ISBN 978-1-338-21981-4

12 11 10 9 8 7 6 5 4 3   17 18 19 20 21 22

Printed in the U.S.A.   40

First Scholastic printing, November 2017

Cover design by Sourcebooks, Inc.
Written by Adam Wallace
The art was first sketched, then painted digitally with brushes designed by the artist.